TWO LOST SOULS

TWO LOST SOULS

RICK POWELL

WRITER

MARIE MOLDOVAN ~ JOE MYKUT

EDITORS

JOE MYKUT

ARTIST

Joseph Mykut -Editor, Cover Images and illustrations

Marie Moldovan - Editor, Publication Layout, and Cover Layout.

TWO LOST SOULS

I Ain't Your Marionette Press, P.O BOX 184, Larder Lake ONTARIO, P0K 1L0, Canada.

FOREWARD

In "Two Lost Souls," Rick Powell dives into the raw vibes of loss and regret. From the foreboding clouds in the opening scene to unspoken words of the characters, Powell crafts a tale that's both relatable and heart-wrenching.

From start to finish, Powell captures the essence of missed opportunities and unfinished business. The dialogue is raw and unfiltered, pulling you into the main character's inner struggles, including hints of past mistakes that might have led to his current situation.

"Two Lost Souls" offers the galactic idea that choices shape our future. Even in life's storms, there's a glimmer of hope and redemption if you're willing to forgive for past slip-ups. If you've ever lost someone and found it hard to let go, this story will hit you right in the feels. Powell's writing offers a complex exploration of grief.

As an editor with I Ain't Your Marionette Press, I've had the privilege of reading and vibing with this story. Reading and offering editorial suggestions for "Two Lost Souls" has been a rewarding experience, letting me see the depth Rick brings to his writing.

Get ready to be moved, to reflect, and maybe even see a bit of your own story within these pages.

~Pita Black of Cranberree Ink

"I stayed with you while you gasped your last breath. It appears I would be the last of your shadowy visitors. My presence was like that of Death, the Inquisitor."

~ Joseph Mykut, The Last Seen Shadow 2021.

Heavy clouds hung in the sky. He pulled up to the gate and heard a low rumble. He wasn't sure if it was the sound the dilapidated engine underneath the hood of his old Pontiac Bonneville made when it was about to stall, or his stomach from not eating all morning.

He could hear the steady creak of the struts as he pulled to a stop. He wanted to be careful of this road; every time he came out here, the asphalt had more potholes than before. It wouldn't do any good to have more damage done to his car, especially after losing his job a few weeks ago.

He put the Bonneville in park and left it running as he took a deep breath, then looked at the woman in the passenger seat. Her simple white dress gave a pleasant contrast to the decrepit interior of the car and the gray sky in the distance. She looked out the passenger window, her slender hands folded in her lap.

"Well, here we are," he said, clearing his throat as if unsure what else to say.

She sighed. "Here we are." She did not turn away from the window. He could just make out her eyes in the reflection of the glass.

He heard a steady rumble in the distance. He glanced out the windshield, feeling a little awkward. "Looks like a storm is coming. I'm glad we got back here in time."

She didn't answer. Her brilliant eyes were moving, taking in the gate that was in her line of vision.

He cleared his throat once more. "Hey, are you okay?"

She turned her head to look at him, no emotion in her eyes, then stared at her delicate hands, white against her white dress. "Yeah," she said softly.

"Thanks for meeting up with me," he said, his voice a little more confident now that she acknowledged him. "We had a pretty good day."

She started rubbing her hands as if she were tensing up to say something. She turned to the window.

He turned the off ignition. *Here we go again.*

The car stopped running, and the silence seemed all the louder. He rubbed the stubble of his unshaven cheek. "I hope it was a good day for you, honey."

"I thought you had work today," she said. She was picking at one of her nails. He swallowed hard and looked at the sky.

"Well, I took the day off. It seemed we were getting together less and less lately." He thought for a moment. "Herb can run the shop on most days by himself. Hell, with that huge superstore that opened a few miles away, we've been slow anyway. No one wants to come to a plumbing supply store when they can get everything they need at a one-stop shopping monster just down the highway."

Her eyes met his. Eyes of the deepest blue. *God, I always loved her eyes.*

"You said last time business was booming. You even had to hire a college kid or two. You said the superstore was bringing in more business with the construction and such." Her voice was hollow and cold.

"Well, it's just that..."

"You lost your job, didn't you?" The sky rumbled, louder than before. He looked into her eyes. She closed them, shook her head, and turned back to look out the window.

"Helen, listen... it's just been hard since..."

"It's been hard for me, too. What are you going to do now, David? You were just getting back on your feet." She abruptly glared at him. "Where are you going to find a job now? Will this car get you there?"

He struggled to say something, shame filling his face.

"You've been drinking again, haven't you?" Helen burted.

He looked down and rubbed his forehead, unsure of what to say. His hand skimmed across the top of his head, avoiding the receding hairline.

"It's just been hard... I miss you," he whispered.

Her shoulders slumped, her anger surrendering to pity. "I know, David. I know."

The sky visible through the windshield was almost filled with the black clouds that loomed overhead. The edges of the glass were starting to mist up from the warmth inside the car as the temperature steadily dropped outside. A stray leaf from the copse of trees on the opposite side of the road blew onto the hood of the car, paused, and tumbled off. He saw the wind buffeting the branches of the trees as if they were urging him to say something.

"Hey, remember that time at the cabin in Michigan when we took the boat out onto that lake? It got so windy, and a large branch fell off that tree and into the water. It was so close to the boat that we got drenched, and you laughed the whole time I was trying to paddle back." He felt a smile come to his face as he looked at her, expectantly.

She looked down in defeat.

He detected a slight chuckle in her throat and cocked his head a little to try to catch her glance. He thought about how, after all these years, her eyes were still dreamy when she recalled a memory from long ago.

Her head snapped up. She gazed out the misting glass, not seeing the clouds, but looking into a day in the past. A day filled with light and sunshine. They were younger then and better at recovering from life's storms.

"When we got back to the cabin, I was laughing so hard because you were paddling as Shaggy did in one of those Scooby-Doo cartoons," she said with a light giggle.

He laughed, heat flushing his cheeks. "Yeah, we almost froze that night, but we managed to keep warm." He winked at her, but she failed to notice.

"You've lost weight," she said, her smile fading. Her gaze never faltered from the sky before her.

He laid back in the seat, knowing his diversion did not work as expected. "Yeah, just a few pounds. Trying to cut out the carbs."

"You didn't eat anything at the restaurant. It was your favorite, too."

"Just wasn't hungry, is all."

"David, listen." She turned to him and looked into his eyes, like a parent advising a child. "You need to take better care of yourself. You have been like this for too long..."

"Helen..."

"...and you need to get yourself together. I've noticed it the last two times we got together, and we can't keep tiptoeing around this three-hundred-pound gorilla in the room. You have to start moving on. What happened, happened. I..."

He slammed his hands on the steering wheel, and lightning flashed on the horizon. "I want you back, dammit!" he shouted.

Helen flinched at his outburst. She turned to the passenger window, retreating into the seat as far away from him as she could. The glass was starting to fog up so he couldn't see her reflection. She put her fingers to her lips. "I know, David, but you realize it can't happen. It's just... too late."

He took a few deep breaths as he gripped the wheel. His eyes drifted shut. "Honey..."

His grip loosened on the wheel as he saw her wipe her cheekbones, her face still looking in the direction of the gate. He hoped it was from the humidity building up in the car but knew otherwise.

"I... I gotta go, David."

Her hand grabbed the door handle; a large drop of water hit the center of the windshield, joined by other large drops. The rain started cascading down the glass from above. She leaned back and sighed, the

atmosphere in the car echoing with
the patter of rain on the roof.

David touched her shoulder.
The coolness of her skin came through
the cotton fabric of her dress.

"Just wait a bit, Helen. Okay?"
he said lightly, pleadingly.

She slowly nodded her head.
"Just a bit, I guess."

They were both sitting there as
sheets of rain poured down onto the
windows, the moments stretching into
hours.

"Why do you keep meeting up
with me?" David whispered.

"You call me, that's why. I
wouldn't feel right if we didn't meet
up." She ran her hand through her
hair and wiped her forehead. She
looked at the sweat beading on his

face as the humidity in the car started to build up. She lowered the window an inch to the frantic sound of the water filling the street and sidewalk beyond. A few drops dampened her sleeve, but she didn't pay attention to it.

"You could have stayed," he said, cocking his head at the gate outside. "Not answered. Not bothered." He wiped the windshield, smearing the window's condensation around.

"I have to make sure you're all right. I hope in some small way that..." She sighed loudly. "Oh, hell, I don't know."

"That I would finally say I'm over you? I found someone else?" David blurted in frustration.

"I just want to make sure you are okay... that's all." Helen whispered.

They both sat without a word, the torrent of water pouring down the glass.

"I am sorry for all I put you through over the years. I was never there. Working. The stress of the bills. The drinking. When you got sick..."

"David, don't. You did all you..."

Lightning flashed, leaving an after-effect in his eyes that he tried to blink away. They could not finish what they were saying. He didn't realize he was still touching her shoulder until he felt the tips of her fingers cover his. Smooth; a coolness he could not define.

"We were a hell of a couple, weren't we?" He looked out at the clouds that were quickly passing. He felt a tinge of disappointment, wishing the storm would linger. Hoping the rain would stall the precious time inside the car.

"Yes, David, we were. In a way, we still are." She looked at him and he closed his eyes. The tender fingertips left his hand and gently stroked his face, the few days' worth of stubble. "You have to let go sometime. We both do."

"I don't want to hold you back."

"I know, David. I know..."

He opened his eyes. The vision of her face blurred, lending her an ethereal quality. The water on the window had yielded to a trickle, revealing an overcast sky; the blackish clouds were now behind them.

"You still need time," she whispered. "Please, get yourself together. For yourself. For me."

"I will."

She gave him a slight smile. The mist cleared from the glass as a soft breeze blew through the opening of the passenger window, bringing with it the scent of wet grass beyond the gate. Hints of zinnias and other flowers began to fill the car.

He tensed up in an attempt to move forward. He looked at the lips he used to kiss... long ago.

He slowly leaned toward her, and she gave him a look that made him pause.

He nodded in understanding and swallowed. The dryness in his throat was evident as he muttered, "I will."

"Good."

He sat back in the seat, wiped his eyes as he rolled down his window, and the humidity left the car. He took a deep breath and looked at the copse of trees across the way, trying not to turn his head when she exited the car.

He keyed the ignition, and the engine coughed once, then started; the seat vibrated, and the car rumbled as he put it in gear.

He heard thunder far away, a kind of forlorn goodbye. He did not look in his rearview mirror as he drove on, a few branches crunching under his worn tires.

Leaves fluttered from the trees across the gate, and one leaf, slick with rain, stuck to the faded cemetery sign and slowly slid off. The fading wind from the storm blew it away, and it tumbled over the grave markers beyond.

The End

ABOUT THE AUTHOR

Rick Powell

Rick Powell is a resident of Oak Forest, Illinois, U.S.A. Rick began writing horror and dark fiction in 2012. His poetic and narrative talents have graced the pages of various publications, including Infernal Ink Magazine and the tantalizing anthology Lustcraftian Horrors: Erotic Stories Inspired by H.P. Lovecraft.

ABOUT THE EDITORS

Joseph Mykut

Joseph Mykut is a native of Alabama. They are an author, artist, illustrator, editor, photographer, and agent. Their artwork and photography are on display internationally in

Ontario, Canada and can be found in the anthologies *3 Amigos Ink and Splatter Lonely Soul in the Darkness, The Way of the Crow and Shattered Psyche*. All anthologies are **I Ain't Your Marionette** Press publications out of Canada. They also authored and illustrated the children's book, "Beautiful Boy", of the same publishing house.

Joseph's art and photography uniquely focuses on the random, seemingly unimportant aspects of the everyday environment surrounding us. They hope this draws attention to the deeper details that express the magic and beauty in the otherwise mundane.

As a member of the LGBTQ2+ community as well as walking the path of Shamanism, they hope to create and represent a more tangible bridge between the physical life experience and the world beyond our physical senses.

Joseph was born and raised in the deep south of the United Sates in what's known as the bible belt. His influences have developed over time to be more of the universe and of spirituality rather than religion.

However, Joseph is an ordained minister with the Universal Life Church as it aligns with his perspective that there is truth found in all religious beliefs as they are all smaller pieces to a greater picture.

They identify as a two spirited being or even multi spirited being and identify with all ideas of the gender spectrum. They believe in the existence of both light and dark or positive and negative energies leaving the truth of who we are to be found in the balance of those energies

Marie Moldovan

Marie Moldovan is a Saskatchewan native and Ontario immigrant. Some would call them a reverse snowbird, who feels most comfortable surrounded by snowcapped mountains.

Nomadic by nature, Marie is multifaceted and has mastered many skills. They dub themselves a jack of many trades and master of some. However, because Marie has acquired a plethora of diplomas spanning the educational spectrum, Marie's mother on the contrary would call them a professional student.

Marie would accredit their adaptability to the training they received as a Canadian Forces medic, and their artistic ability to their family. Both attributes have aided her along their journey from the points of homelessness and despair to the place of stability and optimism Marie has arrived at today.

In 2018, Marie was diagnosed with service-related PTSD, and within the same breath of time became a widow.

Unresolved trauma, and the loss of their husband caused Marie to skirt the edges of insanity. Faced with losing complete touch with reality, they returned to writing and art.

In a sense writing and art saved Marie's life, at least that's their claim. Fortunately, for the world, Marie's choice to embrace creation has led them to captain a new life as a publisher, illustrator, writer and artist.

Marie is the author of **20 years of Winter, Miss Sally Anne** and has currently opened the doors of her own publication organization, aptly named, **I Ain't Your Marionette Press**.

20 Years of Winter is an autobiographical collection of poetry and art. She published it in hopes to make a way for others who have suffered similar traumas to feel safe knowing that they are not alone nor are they to blame for their experiences. *20 Years of Winte*r is Marie's source of empowerment offered to those victims to stand up to their perpetrators and to speak out against victim shaming.

ABOUT THE PUBLISHER

Alas, who are we, marionettes on strings? And what do we stand for, puppeteers of our destiny?

I Ain't Your Marionette distinguishes itself as a stronghold of artistic liberation. At its helm, Marie Moldovan, once a marionette of circumstance, now orchestrates a symphony of narrative freedom. The company's sanctuary breathes life into marionette authors, whose tales of resilience and aspiration paint a vivid tableau of human spirit.

The press's hallmark anthologies, **Shattered Psyche** and **The Way of The Crow**, are more than mere collections; they are immersive experiences that beckon readers to venture beyond the mundane. Each story or visual masterpiece is a declaration of independence, a narrative that defies the norm and invites a reimagining of the world.

The **Voces Animarum** exhibition, alongside the **Shattered Psyche Traveling Showcase** and **Colours of Collaboration**, exemplifies the press's dedication to breaking new ground in literary and artistic expression. These ventures not only elevate the company's stature but also reverberate through the artistic community, transforming subdued creative murmurs into a powerful chorus that resonates far and wide.

FURTHER READING

***

Dive deeper into the captivating worlds crafted by Rick Powell. Each story in this collection explores the boundaries of love, loss, and the supernatural, inviting readers to confront their deepest fears and desires. Whether you're drawn to tales of obsession, apocalyptic nightmares, or chilling mysteries, there's something here for every lover of dark fiction.

Two Lost Souls:

Love, like life, is one of the oldest mysteries. But what happens when love turns into an obsession? When the boundaries between passion and madness blur, and the veil between the supernatural and natural world is cast aside? David believed his bond with his wife Helen was unbreakable, forged in the fires of life's trials. Yet, even the strongest love can be tested by the shadows that lurk in the corners of our hearts—and the darkness of a graveyard.

A Day of Ochre, Ascending:

In this apocalyptic nightmare inspired by Robert W. Chambers' The King in Yellow, a man's ordinary stroll with his dog turns into a nightmare. Each step plunges Walter and Archie deeper into a world of whispered doom. Will they escape, or will the nightmare consume them?

A Banquet of Panacea:

The loss of a child is a wound that never heals. But what if there was a way to move forward, a method so unthinkable it's only whispered about in the shadows? The Richards are living every parent's worst nightmare, their child's life stolen by a remorseless killer. In their darkest hour, they encounter Zhang, a billionaire with a chilling solution: when the justice system fails, he invites the families to a dinner shrouded in mystery and darkness.

Harold:

Frank is a seasoned detective with an uncanny 'feel' for things—a gift that has often guided him through the toughest cases. But this gift comes at a steep price. After years of risking his family and marriage for the job, Frank longs to slow down and reconnect with his loved ones. However, fate has other plans. A mysterious journal lands in his hands, chronicling the twisted crimes of a madman named Harold. Is this a work of fiction, or a chilling true-life account of a delusional killer?

Winston:

Julie lives with her mother in a rundown part of town, struggling to adjust to her mom's new boyfriend, a man she distrusts for many reasons. During a fateful walk home, she encounters Winston, an enigmatic old man whose presence is as captivating as it is mysterious. As their bond deepens, Julie's life begins to change in unimaginable ways. Who is Winston, and what secrets does he hold that could lift Julie out of her adversity? Is he a savior, or a messenger of doom?

Ornament:

The holidays are a time for gathering with friends, family, and loved ones. Blazing fireplaces warm the bodies and hearts of those closest to us, as we share anecdotes of the year's events while the snow and bitter cold blow outside. But for Judith, the cold seeps inside her home, reflecting the turmoil in her life with John. Lies, cheating, and psychological abuse overshadow the season's joy, leaving her without a solution in sight.

Messages:

In a world where technology races forward, leaving yesterday's marvels in the dust, what if someone dared to blend ancient secrets with modern innovations? "Messages" delves into this terrifying possibility. Follow the harrowing journey of a reporter who uncovers the story of a lifetime—a story that could very well be his last. As he digs deeper, he finds himself trapped in a web of dark forces and apocalyptic realities.

A Glimpse Beyond the Veil:

The final book, *A Glimpse Beyond the Veil*, brings together all seven stories. Within this anthology of shadows, secrets writhe through the corridors of forgotten places and sinister whispers shroud the night. Each tale lures readers into the abyss to confront their deepest fears. This collection is a haunting exploration of the human condition and beckons readers to step into a world where reality blurs with the supernatural.

Thank you for your support.